THE LYREBIRD
that is
always too busy to dance

by **PAULINE REILLY**

illustrated by **WILL ROLLAND**

Kangaroo Press

We acknowledge with thanks the help of Dr Alan Lill
and Mr F.N. Robinson.

First published in 1986 by Kangaroo Press Pty Ltd
3 Whitehall Road (P.O. Box 75) Kenthurst NSW 2156
Typeset by G.T. Setters Pty Ltd
Printed in Hong Kong by Colorcraft Ltd

ISBN 0-86417-086-6

Early in the winter,
the wet mountain forests rang
with the song of lyrebirds.

Soon after daybreak,
the lyrebirds glided to the ground
from their roosts in the trees.

3

Each male lyrebird had chosen part of the forest
for himself. In this territory, he scraped up low
mounds of earth, clearing away plants and leaves.

On these mounds, he danced and sang, calling to
the females to mate with him and warning other
males to keep away.

Down in a valley beside a stream, a female lyrebird
had almost finished building her nest.

She stopped to listen.

Then she ran to where the males
    danced and sang.

She watched one male singing on a log.
He sang his own songs
or laughed like a kookaburra
or whistled like a thrush
or made the whipcrack of a whipbird.

He mimicked other birds and
the sound of rustling wings.
All these sounds he made in his throat.

6

Another male was scratching the ground for food.

He stopped when he saw the female lyrebird.

Then, facing her and making clicking sounds,
he walked backwards to his mound.

7

And yet another male danced on his mound
among the ferns.
His tail glowed silvery white
while it quivered and shivered
and shimmered and shook.

8

He jumped as he beat his wings against his body and stepped round the mound to face the female.

She walked on to the mound and they mated.

She knew the male would dance and sing all the winter. There was no time for her to dance but sometimes she sang when her nest was in danger.

She ran back to finish her nest, down in the valley beside the stream.

Each time she sprang up to the nest, she carried little roots or moss.

She laid one dark grey-brown egg.
Each night she incubated the egg, keeping it warm
beneath her belly.

Each day she left the nest, even when
snow lay on the ground.

She had to feed herself.

She raked the ground
or tore open rotting logs
to find worms and insects.

When she left the nest, the egg became cold,
even in the thick bed of feathers that
had fallen from her body.

But the egg soon warmed up when she went back.
She turned to face the entrance,
curling her tail round beside her.
Soon it was bent.

It took nearly seven weeks
for the chick to hatch.
It broke the shell with its egg tooth,
a hard bump on its bill.

The chick was a male
and the mother bird brooded him
to keep him warm.

She clucked when she brought
food to the nest.

When she purred, the chick turned round
and passed his droppings in a little jelly-like sac,
which she took in her bill.

She dropped the sacs in the water farther down the stream or buried them in the ground. Such signs close to her nest could lead other living things to it.

Some of them might harm her chick.

Soon the chick's downy coat had grown
enough to keep him warm. The mother bird could
now spend all day finding food.

She brooded the chick each night,
until he had grown too big for both
of them to fit in the nest.

Then she roosted in a tree above.

One day a raven stood outside the nest.
The chick screeched loudly. The mother bird
ran to protect her chick.

She screeched as she sprang
    at the raven
        making it fly away.

When the young male was nearly seven weeks old,
the mother bird stood below the nest with a bill
full of worms.

He wanted to stay in the nest
but he was hungry.
He glided down to her.

He was almost as big as
she was but his tail was short
and his throat and forehead
were a reddish colour.

Each day they fed, sometimes with other
lyrebirds.
Each night they roosted in trees.

All the lyrebirds moulted in the spring.
Their old feathers fell out and
they preened the new ones to keep them in order.

In the summer and autumn,
the mother bird wandered through the forest,
feeding with the young male.

She would often be watched by adult males.
They sang quietly, raising the wing nearest
to her, courting her, wanting to mate with her.

Early in the winter, the mother bird became too busy to look after the young male.

He joined with other young lyrebirds, most of them under seven years old.

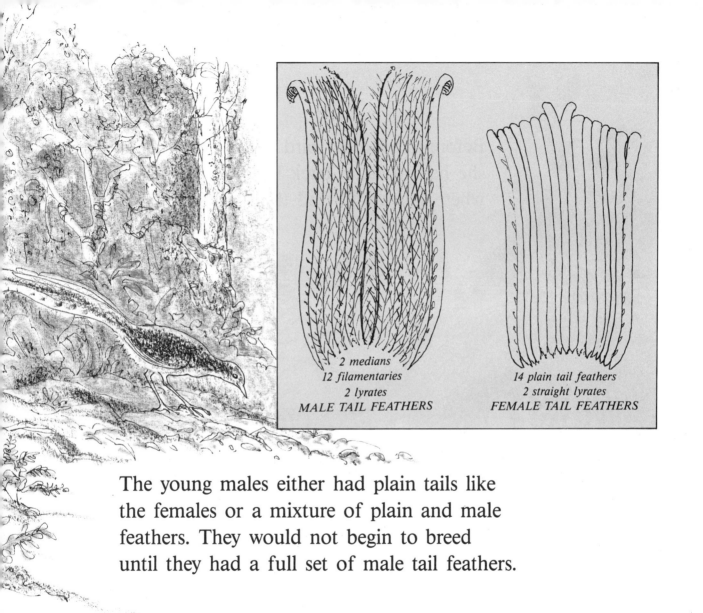

2 medians
12 filamentaries
2 lyrates
MALE TAIL FEATHERS

14 plain tail feathers
2 straight lyrates
FEMALE TAIL FEATHERS

The young males either had plain tails like
the females or a mixture of plain and male
feathers. They would not begin to breed
until they had a full set of male tail feathers.

Before the mother bird could breed again,
she had to claim back her own territory
where she would find the food she needed.

She chased a young female, who had started
to build a nest, and struck at her with her feet.
Feathers flew and the young bird fled.
Then the mother bird pulled the nest to pieces.

This year, the mother bird
built her nest on top
of a treefern.

She reached the nest by springing from branch
to branch of nearby trees.

Then she glided
back
to the ground.

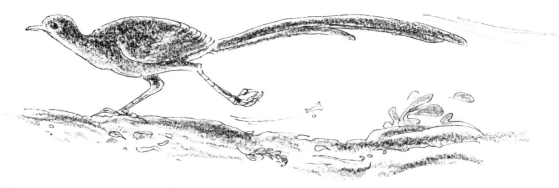

She ran to where the male lyrebirds danced and sang.
When she had chosen one and mated,
  she ran back to finish her nest,

    . . . to incubate her egg

      . . . to care for her new chick

    until next year, early in the winter . . .

SHE WAS ALWAYS TOO BUSY TO DANCE.

The scientific name for the Superb Lyrebird
is *Menura novaehollandiae* (Men-you-́rah no-vi-holl-and-́ee-i),
which means 'mighty or wonderful tail of New Holland'.
New Holland was the name once given to Australia.

Albert's Lyrebird

Superb Lyrebird

Lyrebirds live only in Australia.
There is only one family and it has two species:
the Superb Lyrebird and Albert's Lyrebird.
They are very much alike.

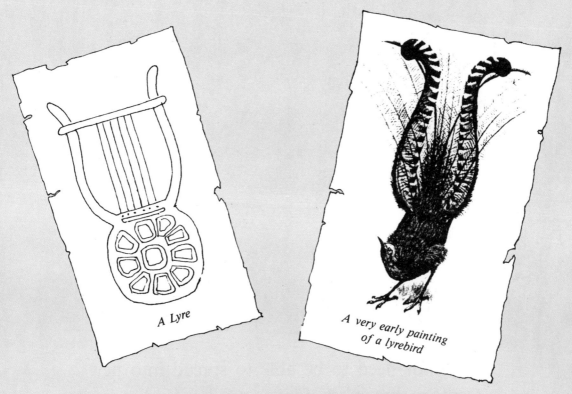

A Lyre

A very early painting of a lyrebird

When early scientists looked at dead lyrebirds, they thought the tail looked like a lyre, a musical instrument. But living birds do not hold their tails that way.

Lyrebirds need to be able to spread into new
territory, but when forests are cleared,
they have nowhere to live.
In the wild, they have been known to live for
more than twenty years.